SHARING THE MOUNTAIN

The Second Y

Copyright 2017 by J. L. Roberts. All rights reserved.

Table Of Contents

Introduction 2
Chapter 1: Spring 1980 5
Chapter 2: Summer 1980 28
Chapter 3: Autumn 1980 48
Chapter 4: Winter 1980 76
Conclusion 94

Introduction

I have seen a lot in my lifetime, but the one thing that still haunts me today was when my family and I lived in the mountains of the Appalachians. My husband Jake and I wanted to settle down with our two children on a farm that we purchased in 1979. We purchased a little piece of paradise that consisted of a farmhouse, with a barn, and eight acres of land. It was our paradise. I fell in love with the old farmhouse the first time I saw it.

Our dream was to have a full working farm to produce enough income so that Jake could quit his job in the city and work full time at the farm and to be close to me and the children.

We were working hard on getting

enough farm animals and growing wheat to sell to produce enough income to support our family. It was demanding work, but very rewarding and the thought of Jake being able to quit his job in the city made me work harder.

As Jake and I were clearing the trees off the land to plant the wheat, more weird and unusual things started happening around the property, and the more I was concerned about a creature that might be lurking in the woods that I never believed existed.

As I am writing this, reminiscing back to those days, with my children so small and I was young, it is a bittersweet memory to remember for the rest of my life. But as time goes by ever so swiftly and the children have grown up and moved out of the house, it gives me time to think of how I put my precious babies in danger so many times when we were living at the farm. As the saying goes "hindsight is 20/20" and if I knew then what I know now, we would never have purchased the property.

But we did purchase the property, and we did live there, and we did have great times that are special, along with terror and nightmares that would be so overwhelming that I just wanted to move so far away from the mountains and never go back.

This book is a continuation of the first book, "Sharing the Mountain with Bigfoot, the First Year". If you haven't read the first book, please do so for that's where it all begins.

I will begin this book in the spring, as I did with the first book, and to think back, I don't recall anything happening around the first of the year 1980. It seems like after the first snowfall that happened in the winter of 1979; everything was quiet and peaceful. Is it because the elusive creature would migrate to warmer areas during winter? I don't know, but research does say that they do migrate to warmer areas in search of food.

Chapter 1: Spring 1980

We have made it through our first winter on the mountain. Spring had sprung, and the snow was finally melting away. I was anxious for the warmer weather and working in my garden, playing with the children in the back yard, and wearing sandals again.

Jake was still working at his job in the city, which month by month, we were getting closer for him to retire from that job and work full time at the farm. In my mind though, it was taking so long to build the farm up for him to quit.

In the year 1980, we purchased more farm animals and cleared off more land to plant wheat and corn. We cleared the land on the back of our property for the corn. With the wheat, we plowed the ground where we planted it the last year.

One Saturday morning, I awaken to a beautiful sight. The sun was shining brightly through our bedroom window, flooding the room with sun rays and the feeling of spring.

I got out of bed and went to Cody's and Emma's bedrooms to see if they were awake yet. Surprisingly, both children were still asleep. I went down to the kitchen to start breakfast for Jake and the children. I opened the curtains in the kitchen to let the natural light and the warmth of the sun in.

It was a beautiful day and I was in a great mood. I wanted to get out of the house as soon as I could.

"Today will be a wonderful day to get out of the house and explore" I said to myself, staring out the kitchen windows.

"What are you thinking about?" Jake asked while coming into the kitchen, dressed in his farming clothes and carrying his boots.

"Isn't it a beautiful day?" I said, pointing toward the kitchen window.

"Yes, it is" Jake said as he sits down at the kitchen table. "I am going to go purchase a few goats today. John is coming with me and Karen wants to come over for a visit."

That made me happy. John and Karen, our neighbors, had been the best of friends that anyone could have. We had grown close to them and considered them our family. Of course, they were much older than Jake and me but that didn't make any difference to us.

After breakfast, John and Karen pulled up to the house. Shortly, John and Jake were busy getting the trailer hooked onto the truck in order to go purchase some goats. Karen and I started our visit in the front room of the house and then took the children out to the back yard. We wanted to enjoy the fresh air, and the sun shining on my face felt amazing.

Our conversation consisted of the usual "How are you? What are you planting in the garden this year? What kinds of flowers do you have?" And, "where did you get those sandals? I love them!"

We were having the best time visiting with each other when suddenly, Karen seemed to get quiet and started staring out into the woods. I noticed the strange look on her face when she seemed to snap out of the staring moment and looked at me. She gave me a small smile.

"Is there something bothering you, Karen?" I asked.

"No, nothing of importance," Karen said as she took a puff of her cigarette that was burning between the fingers of her right hand.

I could still see the worried look in her eyes as she looked away from me, blew the smoke out of her lungs and started watching the children play.

I didn't want to push her to tell me what she was worried about, but curiosity was getting the best of me.

"You know you can talk to me about anything, and I am a good listener and a shoulder to cry on if you need me," I said to Karen as I put my hand on her shoulder.

"Thank you, sweetie," Karen said as she looked away and into the woods once again.

"I just don't know how to tell you about..."

Just about that time, Jake was coming up the driveway with the new farm animals, blowing the horn to alert us that he had arrived.

Karen and I, along with the children started walking toward the front of the house to meet Jake and John. As they get out of the truck, Jake bent down to pick Emma up and walked to the back of the trailer to show her the goats. Both Cody and Emma were delighted to see the new farm animals.

As everyone had their attention on the new animals, watching them being unloaded and put into the fenced area closer to the front yard, we didn't notice the activity going on in the back part of the property.

As Karen and I were keeping the children away from the men working, I started to hear a familiar sound that I heard back in the summer of the last year. I turned around to face the back of the house when suddenly, I heard a "Whoop" sound coming from the far end of the property just inside the tree line.

I looked at Karen, and she was looking in the same direction where I was with a very concerned look on her face.

"Did you hear that?" I asked Karen, still focused on the concerned look she was making.

"Yes, I did hear that," She said as she looked at John.

John looked at Karen then closed the gate of the goat pen, then said that they had to be going.

Karen and John said their goodbye's as we watched them drive down our long driveway.

As I watched our neighbors drive down the driveway, I gathered the children and started moving toward the house. I started praying that what I just heard in the back of the house was just a bird and not what Jake said he saw back in the winter.

As soon as I stepped into the house, I put Emma down in the front living room and headed to the back door to make sure it was locked and then closed the kitchen window curtains.

Later that evening when dinner was finished, and the children had their baths, I wanted to talk to Jake about the noise that I heard in the back. Since we haven't had any kind of odd occurrences around the property for a while, I was hoping that Jake could give me an explanation of the noise and relieve my worries.

"I didn't hear anything, darling, I was busy putting the goats in the fence," Jake said when I asked him about it.   "Karen heard it too, so I'm not the only one," I said as I sat on the sofa, holding a magazine that I had wanted to flip through.

"Karen was acting a little strange today and wanted to tell me something, but never did. Do you know anything about it?"

"No, and don't worry about it, Jada" Jake said as he turned the television on to watch the news.

I know Jake. When he says Jada, not darling or sweetie, I know that he is getting frustrated and I stopped talking. But that still didn't help me of thinking that the unknown creature that had been lurking around the property last year may be back.

I put the magazine down and settled down to watch the news with Jake and tried not to think about it. The next thing I knew, it was bedtime, and I was very tired. I needed rest.

The following weekend, Jake wanted to get started clearing the trees from the back of the property to plant the corn. After his daily chores with the farm animals, he would get the chainsaw out and the tractor to start in the fields.

During the week, I would try to have all the laundry finished, and the house cleaned so I could help Jake with clearing the brush for the corn that we would sell in the fall. It was an exciting time because I knew when we had all the wheat and corn planted and then harvested and sold in the fall, we would be that much closer for Jake to quit his job and stay at home with me and I knew Jake also felt the same way. He did not like his job in the city, but it did pay the bills and get us the necessities we needed to live.

As time went on, the days were getting longer and warmer. We needed to hurry and get the land cleared and the fields planted before the spring rains began.

I had to wait to help Jake in the fields until after lunch, and the children were down for their naps. When the children were asleep, I grabbed my old shoes off the back porch and headed down to the back of the property where Jake was working. I got about half way to the field when suddenly, I smelled the same putrid odor I have smelled before. My blood ran cold, and a chill went straight up my spine! I turned around as fast as I could and ran back to the house to make sure the door in the front was locked. I don't know why I thought of the front door being locked when the smell was by Jake, I had a feeling of nothing else but protecting my children.

When I reached the back door and ran

through the kitchen, then the front living room, I noticed as soon as I got closer to the front door, the terrible smell was getting stronger again. I started to panic! I felt like I was in slow motion trying to get to the front door to lock it. Finally, I locked the front door, but the smell was still there. I peered out the front bay window onto the porch to see if there were anything out there. I couldn't see anything, but that didn't mean nothing was there.

As I was looking out of the window in the front of the house, Jake came in the back door rushing to the front living room where I was standing, going for the shotgun right beside me. I looked at Jake, and the look on his face was a mixture of concern and fright.

"My God, is it back?" I asked Jake in a panicked voice.

"Stay in the house Jada, lock the door behind me," Jake said as he goes out to the front porch.

I obeyed what Jake had told me. My head was spinning, and I had to sit down on the sofa before I fell on the floor.

After what seemed like hours gone by, Jake came back to the house carrying his shotgun.

The children were in the living room with me as Jake came up onto the front porch and I jumped up to unlock the door to let him in.

"What is it?" I asked while Jake was putting the shotgun back into its place, hanging on the wall by the front door.

Jake sits down in his rocker and leaned back, puts his head back and sighed.

I waited for about a minute before I said anything else to Jake. I had to know what is going on and I started to get frustrated at him for taking so long to talk to me.

"Please tell me, I need to know something!" I said as he looked at me in an aggravated stare.

"I don't know darling" Jake said as he helped Emma climb up to his lap. "All I know is that I have to get the fields plowed soon so we can have enough corn and wheat to sell by fall. This is getting ridiculous, and I'm going to ignore it. It hasn't messed with anything around the farm, so maybe it is just passing through."

With that said, I was still in denial of what Jake had told me what this creature was. I cannot believe that there was a real Bigfoot creature stomping around in the mountains. It was unbelievable to me.

The next day, Jake got up earlier in the morning and started plowing the fields for the planting of wheat. I must have been very tired, for I was the last one up and out of bed that morning.

I went to the children's room and to my surprise, both Cody and Emma were not in their rooms. I rushed downstairs to find where they may be and was shocked that they were in the living room watching cartoons on the television.

That's one of the many reasons that I love Jake; he must have told the children not to leave the living room until I was awake. The children would listen to him because he would be stern when necessary.

I went to the kitchen to pour a cup of coffee and sit down at the kitchen table. I heard the tractor working in the fields that we were clearing for the corn. I wanted so much to go help Jake with the clearing of the corn field, but what had happened the day before, I was still a little spooked.

I got up from the kitchen table with my cup of coffee and go out to the back porch to sit in the rocker. As I watched Jake move some of the cut trees out of the fields with his tractor, I thought of how nice it would be when Jake's full time job will be the property and farm.

As I sat on the back porch, daydreaming of our future, and watching Jake clear the brush in the field, I saw something move close to the tree line and behind a brush pile next to where Jake was with his tractor. I tried to focus on what it was when suddenly, a huge log was thrown up and over the brush pile and it hit Jake, throwing him off his tractor.

I panicked! I dropped my coffee cup on the porch, spilling the remaining coffee all over the porch, and started running down to the field to where Jake was lying on the ground. I started praying that Jake was okay and not worried about what had just thrown a huge log at him.

As I was getting closer to Jake, the smell of rotten flesh and feces hit me in the face and I started to vomit, but I could not stop running until I knew that Jake was going to be okay. I knew he was injured but to what extent, I didn't know.

I finally reached Jake. He was still on the ground but sitting up holding his head. There was blood coming from a gash on the side of his head, and his breathing was a little labored. I reached him and noticed that his arm was twisted in a way that was not normal.

"My God, Jake," I said with bated breath, my heart beating in my ears and trying to help him up to his feet.

"I have to get you to the hospital," I said

trying my best to carry him to the house.

"I'll be alright, sweetie" Jake said, limping but walking toward the house with my arms holding him up as best as I could.

But your arm must be broken" I said as I looked up to the house and saw that the children were running toward us in the field.

Panic filled my soul again! The children were out of the house and in danger with the unknown creature that was so close to us that it could easily run out of the woods and take one of my babies. My legs started to get shake and became weak.

"Cody! Get Emma into the house now!" I screamed, trying to walk as fast as my legs would go while being a human brace for Jake to lean on.

Cody obeyed my order and turned around and led Emma back toward the house.

Finally, we made it to the back porch, and I helped Jake up the steps and into the kitchen. The children were looking at their daddy with concern showing in their eyes. I sat Jake down at the kitchen table and ran to the phone that was on a small table in the living room.

The first phone number that I could remember was John and Karen's. I dialed the number and Karen answered.
I don't really remember what was said, but before I knew it, John and Karen were on the front porch coming into the living room.

Karen walked straight to Jake and looked at the gash on his head. Then she examined his arm.

"Looks like you may need to see a doctor for both your head and arm." She said as she was still checking Jake for other injuries.

"We will stay here with the children if you want to take him into town to see the Doctor." Karen said to me as she was still looking at Jake.

"Thank you, Karen" was the only thing I could think of while I was getting my purse and things that I needed to go into town to see the doctor.

John helped Jake into our truck and we both headed down our driveway to go down the mountain to the city.

We arrived at the doctor's office, and Jake's injuries were more severe than we had thought. He had to have stitches to close the gaping wound that was on the side of his head. As for his arm, he did have an Oblique bone fracture and had to be fitted with a cast.

While I was waiting for the doctor to finish bandaging Jake's head and arm, I couldn't help but feel safer in town than at home in the woods. I was thinking if only we lived in the city, we would not be having these terrible issues. I also was anxious to get back home to the farm where my children were waiting for us. To say the least, I was a nervous wreck and could hardly wait for all this to be over. It seemed that I was having the worse nightmare that I could ever imagine.

By the time Jake and I left the city, it was getting late in the evening, and I would have to drive up the mountain in the dark. I hated driving at night on the country roads because of the abundant deer in the woods and crossing the roads. Seems that they would wait until a vehicle was in sight before they would cross the road, leaving the driver with no option but to hit the deer.

    We made it back to the house safely, and I pulled the truck as close to the front porch steps as I could get for Jake to be helped up to the porch and into the house. As soon as I opened Jake's passenger side door, John was there to help him up into the house. I followed them into the house to find that Karen had the children fed and bathed, and dinner was waiting on the stove for us, and everything was taken care of around the house. Thank you, John and Karen. What wonderful neighbors we had.

    With the children in bed and trying my best to make Jake as comfortable as possible, I said goodnight to our neighbors and walked them to the front door. After shutting the front door and making sure all the doors were locked, I headed upstairs to bed. I was exhausted.

With Jake being injured and the doctors' orders were for him to rest and 'take it easy for a few days,' I had a lot of chores to do. Not only my chores but some of Jake's chores too.

The only good thing about the accident was Jake couldn't go to work with his arm broken, and he had to stay at home with me. That made me feel safer with all the weird things that were going on at that time.

The next day when Jake woke up and wanted to eat breakfast, I sat down beside him at the kitchen table and told him what I saw the day before and how that log came to hit him on the head and knocked him off the tractor.

Needless to say, he didn't see it and told me I was wrong. He said that accidents happen all the time when farming and that log fell off the big brush pile and hit him. With everything I had in me as far as disagreeing with him, I was wrong, and he was right. I gave up and told him to believe what he wanted, and that was the end of that argument. But I do know what I saw that threw the log at Jake. I guess it didn't matter so much as it did to try and get Jake well again and back to doing what he needed to do.

Now that I was the only one that could take care of the animals on the farm for a few days. Jake showed me where all the feed was for the different animals that we had.

He would go out to the barn with me and would try his best to help me feed the hogs, horse, goats, and chickens. It was very challenging work for one person, and I had a renewed respect for Jake for the demanding work that he did every day around the farm.

After all the animals were fed and watered, the laundry and food cooked for Jake and the children, I was so exhausted and ready for a long bath and a good night's rest.

I put the children to bed, and I was headed for my comfortable bed and pillow. It was getting warm in the house, and I wanted some fresh air in the bedroom. I get up out of bed and open the window when I heard Cody open his bedroom door and came out running into our bedroom.

"Mommy, the goats are loud, and I can't sleep," Cody said as he waited for me to follow him back to his room.

I followed Cody back to his bedroom to see what he was talking about. Cody's bedroom was a little warm, and I wanted to open the window to let in some cool night air. As I approached the window in his room, I could hear the goats bleating and running frantically around in their fenced area.

I opened the window, and the goats were so loud that I was surprised that Jake wasn't awakened by them. I stood by the window looking out to see if I could see anything that could be frightening them but could see nothing.

After a few moments had passed, the goats started to calm down and huddle around at the far end of the fence. I stood there looking out the window long enough that the goats started lying down and being quiet.

I put Cody back into his bed and kissed him goodnight, for I was headed to bed for some much-needed rest.

The next day was a repeat of the day before. Jake would follow me and would try to help me with feeding and watering the animals. When we got to the goat fence to feed them, Jake started looking at the side of the fence that was the closest to the tree line. The fence on top of the wires was bent almost in half. Jake and I started to investigate the fence and noticed that where the fence was bent down, the leaves on the ground were disturbed as if someone was walking on them or dragging something.

Jake turned his attention to the goats and started to count them. I never thought about how many goats that he had purchased and since I was so busy while we had the goats, I never thought about counting them myself.

"How many do we have? I asked Jake as he finished counting.

"Seven, one is missing," Jake said as he started looking toward the tree line. "I bought eight."

The more I thought about this creature that was coming around our farm, the more frightened I became. So many questions were running through my mind that I knew I would never have answers to. The biggest one "Is it safe to settle down here on our little piece of paradise with a creature that some people call Bigfoot?"

Chapter 2: Summer 1980

Summer months were the most challenging months of the year. There was no relief from the hot and humid days, and the nights were just as warm. No rain in the forecast and the fields were screaming for water.

Jake was over his injury and back to work at his job in the city and taking care of his chores at the farm. He was trying to think of ways to come up with enough water to wet the fields of corn and wheat. I let out a little chuckle when he told me that we were going to have to haul some water from the river that was flowing at the end of our property to water the fields.

"Do you have any other ideas?" Jake asked, knowing what my answer would be.

"No, but how are we going to do that?" I asked in a somewhat aggravated tone.

"I will call John to see he can help. Maybe he has a few ideas we can try" Jake said as he headed to the phone in the living room.

To my surprise, Jake and John came up with a plan. I don't know how far the river was to the fields, but Jake and John laid down small plastic pipes that stretched from the river to the fields. Somehow, they diverted the water to go into the pipe, up to the fields and it started watering the wheat field. We had to carry the water to the corn field, which was back breaking work, but our fields were watered, and we were happy.

A few days after Jake and John put the pipes together, and a little water was trickling out of them from the river, I was loading the laundry basket and carrying it out to the line to hang the clothes to dry. When suddenly, I started to hear a weird knocking sound. It sounded like something hollow hitting a tree. Then I would hear a high-pitched whistle coming from the tree line close to the path that goes down to the river and where Jake and John had put the pipes. It was made into a pattern. Three knocks, then whistle. Repeat. That went on for about five times. I swiftly hung the clothes on the line and went back into the house where I felt safer.

When Jake came home from work, I told him about what I had heard. He goes out to where the pipes were coming in to the fields and checked to see if the water was still flowing through the pipes. It wasn't long before I saw Jake coming back from the fields carry a piece of the pipe in his hand.

"The whole pipeline is destroyed!" Jake exclaimed in a very strong and frustrated manner. "Now our crops don't have any water!" he said as he threw the piece of pipe on the ground.

The next half hour after that was something I have never seen in Jake before. His temper flared, and I saw a man that has had enough and was ready to do something that he may regret.

I tried to calm his frustration, but it was

to no avail. The more I tried, the angrier he would get. I gave up trying, and finally, he calmed down long enough to tell me he was going to go into the woods and not come out until this situation was solved.

To my relief, I looked down our driveway and saw John and Karen driving up to the house for a visit. As John was getting out of the truck, I came to his side and tried to tell him what was going on. He looked at Jake and said he would help him and we went to the barn where we saw Jake heading to when they pulled up.

Karen came and stood beside me as I was watching John walk to the barn.

"Everything will be okay sweetie," Karen said as she put her arm around my shoulder and guided me toward the house and to the children that were waiting on the front porch for me.

"I hope so, Karen, but at this point, I am ready to just give up on everything," I said as I turned my focus on to my children watching us on the front porch.

"Let's go inside and relax and wait for the guys to come back. John and I have something that we want to talk to you and Jake about, that's why we came over today" Karen was saying this as she led me to the front porch steps.

"What is it? Can you tell me now?" I asked as I looked into her eyes and could see the concern she was holding.

"I promised John I would not say anything until you both were present and John could help explain," Karen said as she stooped down to pick Emma up onto her lap.

"Great! More bad news. Just what I need at this moment" I thought to myself as I sat down hard on the sofa and sighed, thinking of what else could possibly go any more wrong.

As the time ticked by, the anticipation of when the men would be back and what Karen and John wanted to tell us was wearing me down to exhaustion.

I went to the kitchen and fixed Karen and I a cup of coffee. I bring the two cups of coffee back to the front living room where Karen was reading a book to Cody and Emma.

"I wonder what is taking Jake and John so long to come back home?" I asked in a confused manner as I handed Karen the cup of coffee.

"I'm sure they will be back soon, please don't worry so much. They will be okay."

Thank God for Karen. She always knew how to calm my nerves when I needed it. With her kind words and motherly wisdom, I would hang on to her every word and knew she was telling me the truth, even if she was a little unsure herself of what she would say. But it didn't matter to me. If she said the men would come home safe, then I knew that they would come home safe.

It was now dark when we heard Jake and John coming up the steps of the front porch. Karen and I jumped up and rushed to the front door to unlock it so the men could come inside.

The look on their faces seemed of

frustration and exhaustion, but that didn't stop me from demanding answers of what they did or found in the woods. Not only that, but John and Karen had something to tell Jake and me, and it was important enough for them to drive over to our house that night.

The children were in bed by the time Jake and John was settled and comfortable on the living room furniture. I served them both with coffee and homemade cookies that I had baked earlier that day.

I was getting ready to flood the men with questions when suddenly Karen started talking to John about why they had come over for their visit.

"Well darling, should I start off by telling them what we have known for a very long time now?" Karen said as she stared at John as he ate the last cookie on his plate.

Before John could say anything, I looked at Jake, and he stopped eating and was staring at Karen.

"Go ahead Karen and tell them" is all

that John said as he puts the plate down on the end table that was closest to his rocker.

Karen waited for about a minute before she started talking as if she was trying to think of the right words to say. Finally, she looked up from the floor that she was staring at, facing Jake, she started talking.

"It started about ten years ago. We still had our youngest child living with us. She was a teenager then and ready to go to college. She would walk our long driveway in the evening for exercise as she was always worried about her figure. One evening, while she was walking up the driveway, I was watching her from our front porch when suddenly, a big black figure started walking very fast out of the woods and toward her. She noticed the figure about the same time as I did and started to run back toward the house. I started screaming and yelling for my daughter to run as fast as she could, but the figure was gaining on her. It had to be about seven to eight feet tall. It had very long legs, long arms, and covered with hair.

I started to run toward my daughter, screaming, but I knew I would not get to her before the creature would and I started praying for a miracle. That miracle came as a shot rang out from John's shotgun. That blast scared the creature, and it stopped chasing my daughter and ran back into the woods. She was safe from the monster for that moment.

After that incident, things around our house started to get weird. Just like they are here. Our pigs started to disappear, and we would find footprints all over the farm. The chickens were disappearing fast, and our barn was practically destroyed. Everything that we tried to do to keep the creature away, the more it would destroy our property, except in the winter months when the temperature would drop to freezing. Seems that the creature would not bother us then.

"When John came home with about three dogs one spring morning, things seemed to settle down for a while. I guess it was because the weather was still a little cold, but when it became warmer, even with the dogs, the creature would come back and terrorize us. Finally, after about four years and five dogs running around the property, the creature that we call and is known as Bigfoot, left and never came back. That is until you bought this property, we thought that it was gone for good" Karen said as she looked at Jake, then turned and looked at me, not knowing if she should continue her story for what our reaction would be.

I was stunned. Not only did John and Karen know what was going on around our property, but they also lived the terror of the creature at their property.

"You knew what was going on around here and didn't tell us sooner?" I heard Jake blurt out, with an angry tone in his voice.

"We wanted to tell you, but we were hoping that this thing would disappear and move on before we had to tell you. And we really didn't think that you would believe us if we did tell you" John said as he took another sip of his coffee.

"We would have believed you, John" Jake said looking at John, noticeably upset.

"As a matter of fact, I saw it last winter and knew what I was looking at. Then after the first snowfall, we didn't have any problems with it after that. I still can't believe that you didn't say anything about it while we went out in the night looking for this thing. John and I could have been killed," Jake exclaimed as he sat close to the edge of his rocker staring at John.

It was getting late and John and Karen needed to return to their home, both Jake and I forgave our neighbors for not telling us sooner of what they knew about the creature that was coming around our property. How could we not forgive them? They have been the best of friends we could possibly have hoped for.

After John and Karen had left the house, I started locking all the doors and started moving upstairs to go to bed. As I passed Cody's room, I heard him call out to me in a faint voice.

I went into his room to check on him. I went to his bed, and he told me he was thirsty. I put my hand on his head to brush his hair back and noticed that his skin was very hot. I started touching his face and noticed he was burning hot.

I rushed back down to the kitchen to find the thermometer that was kept in the kitchen cabinet with the homemade first aid kit. After grabbing the thermometer and taking the stairs back up to Cody's room, I took his temperature. It read 101 degrees Fahrenheit! My baby boy was sick!

Being exhausted with the day's activities, and then one of my children was sick that night, all I wanted to do was break down and cry. I had as much drama as I could stand. Something had to change. I needed a break from the farm.

The next few days after was an exhausting experience. While taking care of my sick son and trying to get all the daily chores that I could do, I was left feeling worn down and defeated. Cody wasn't getting over his sickness as soon as I thought he should and every day that passed made me that much more worried about him. His fever would break and then come back a little higher each time. By the third day with his elevated temperature, it was time to visit the doctor.

Jake and I loaded Cody and Emma into the truck and drove down the mountain and into town to the doctor's office.

As we were patiently waiting to see the doctor in the cramped waiting area, I saw that someone had left a local newspaper on the coffee table sitting in front of me. I picked it up and turned it over to the front page, and something caught my eye. In big letters on the front page read "Family Terrorized in the Mountains!" My heart dropped into my stomach!

I started reading the article and realized that we were not the only family who had been visited by this unknown animal. How many families know about this creature?

Now I felt a little better about it because other people besides us and our neighbors knew about this animal lurking in the woods and I knew I wasn't going crazy.

Just before we were called to go back to see the doctor, the town Sheriff came through the door. Jake gets up to shake his hand. They started with small talk about how the sheriff was doing and if everything was going well in the city. I wanted some answers about this so called creature that I knew was a Bigfoot. I didn't want to interrupt their conversation, but I was getting very impatient to ask him questions before we had to go in the back where the doctor was.

"I'm sorry to interrupt your conversation, but do you know anything about this?" I asked, holding up the newspaper and pointing to the article.

The Sheriff started walking toward me, and I handed him the newspaper. While he was looking at the article, he started nodding his head and started to tell us the story.

Jake and I stood there listening to the

Sheriff while he was telling us about the article that I had just read. But then the conversation started with another family that had been affected by this creature.

"You know that was the main reason that the family that lived closer to your farm had just disappeared, leaving all their possessions at the house," he said as he looked at Jake and me.

"Seems like the animal scared them away, according to some children that go to school with the older siblings of the family, and to this day, no one had seen that family around town or anywhere else. There is an ongoing investigation about what had happened to that family," the sheriff said as he handed me back the newspaper, tipped his hat in a goodbye motion, turned and walked to the receptionist at the end of the waiting area.

I was shocked at what the sheriff had told us. The family that we had thought was trying to harass us and scaring us from our property, had been harassed themselves by an unknown creature. They were harassed so bad that they left their house and all their belongings behind. All I could think about was what if it gets so bad around our property that we had to leave as our neighbors had done?

    At that moment, the doctor was ready to see Cody. My attention turned to Cody and the realization of why we were here in the first place. But my mind was reeling from what the Sheriff had told us, and I had more questions that I needed answered.

    After our visit to the doctor's office and Cody had diagnosed with an upper respiratory infection, and with bottles of medication to fight it, we were driving back up into the mountains toward our farm.

    As we were turning into our driveway and driving up to the house, the truck came to a sudden stop. I looked at Jake and noticed that he was staring straight ahead in the yard. I looked to where he was staring and noticed that our chickens were out of their fenced area and running around in the yard in front of the house.

Jake, being a man of few words, drove the truck up to the front porch for me to get the children into the house and come back out to help him gather the chickens and put them back into the fence where they belong. After getting the children into the house, I went out to the front porch and down the steps to find one of the chickens pecking the ground. I tried to sneak up on it to grab it to take back to the coop. Just as I was about to grab the chicken, Jake comes around the side of the house and tells me to let it go. I looked at him, confused.

"The chicken coop is destroyed," Jake said as he started walking up the steps, his body language telling me that he was tired and disgusted.

"What? How?" was the only thing I could say as I followed Jake into the house and made sure the door was shut and locked behind me.

I went to the back of the house to the kitchen to look out the windows where I could see the chicken coop. To my surprise, the coop was demolished! The fence was lying on the ground, and the wooden planks that were used to make the coop were strewn all over the back of the yard.

By that time, I felt defeated, and I was ready to give up on the farm. There was no way, in my mind, that we could compete with a Bigfoot that wanted to destroy everything that we had on the property. I couldn't see how we could stop this creature and before long, we wouldn't have anything left that wasn't destroyed.

I closed the kitchen window curtains and went to the front living room to check on Cody where he was lying on the sofa. To my relief, his fever was lower, and the color on his face was coming back and seemed like he was feeling better.

Before I sat down beside Cody, I turned on the television to watch the show "Alf," while Jake went upstairs to take a shower.

I was getting comfortable on the sofa with my two children next to me watching the silly show that was Cody's and Emma's favorite thing to watch on television when suddenly, I heard someone walking on the front porch! I knew Jake was upstairs taking a shower and we were not expecting any company.

My body stiffened, and I didn't know what to do. I waited to see if there would be a knock on the door when suddenly I saw a huge shadow going past the bay window. I started to panic, and then I heard Jake coming down the stairs. I jumped up from the sofa and met him at the foot of the stairs, telling him in a panic voice that someone was on the front porch.

Jake rushed to the front door, after he grabbed his shotgun, and jerked the door open.

Nothing was on the porch! Jake went out of the house and onto the porch, down the steps and around the side of the house, toward the barn. He finally came back into the house and told me that he didn't see anything, but the animals were acting a little spooked, but nothing was out of place that Jake could tell.

"Are you sure you heard something walking on the porch? Jake asked as he put the shotgun back down.

"Yes, I know I heard something and I saw a huge shadow in the bay window. I know I'm not going crazy, Jake." I said as I gathered the children and started up the stairs to put them to bed.

While I was putting the children to bed, I started thinking about why Jake would have asked me that question, and I realized that something was different. I didn't smell the appalling stench that we would smell when the creature was around. When Jake opened the front door to go out, there was only the fresh night air coming through the door. Was I going crazy? Was I so paranoid about it that every sound or noise that I heard I thought was the creature? Can I live here with my family any longer? Something needed to change.

Chapter 3: Autumn 1980

The summer was hot and miserable, but it had finally come to an end. Autumn was here, and the cooler winds were blowing in the fresh air and cooling the house, making it bearable to live in.

The last month of summer had little to no rain making the fields and ground dry and dusty. The fields were in bad shape but it was getting closer to be harvested.

Jake was still working at his job in the city but was becoming impatient and wanted to take some time off to gather the corn and wheat. I was happy when he told me he was taking some time off from his work to tend to the fields.

"That's a wonderful idea," I said in an overly excited voice that made Jake chuckle.

"I'm ready for this farm to be my full-time job. We'll see how much money the fields bring in this year to know if I can quit my job next year" Jake said as he put his boots on and started walking out the back door heading toward the barn to start the tractor.

"I pray that it does," I said to myself, watching him walk to the barn through the kitchen window.

My attention turned to the children that were running to the table where their breakfast was waiting on them. Both Cody and Emma were in cheerful moods, wanting to go outside to play after breakfast.

"Let's go into town and buy some pumpkins to decorate the front of the house," I said as I looked excited at the children.

The children were thrilled to hear about going into town and after breakfast I gathered what I needed to take with me, put the children in the truck, kissed Jake goodbye for the day, and drove down the driveway toward the small city in the valley.

It was so nice to get away from the farm for a while, and I enjoyed shopping and seeing other people. I took the children to the park to play for a while, then we went to the produce shop for Cody and Emma to pick out two pumpkins, then to the grocery store for our necessities.

The day was packed full of fun and exciting things to do, but it was getting late. It was time to go back to the farm to prepare dinner. Jake would be getting hungry, and the children needed their baths.

As I was driving back up the mountain, I had an uneasy feeling about something. I didn't know if it was because we were leaving the city or if it was something to do with the farm.

While I was driving up the dark curvy mountain, with my mind being boggled with all kinds of "what if" questions, when suddenly, right in front of the truck appeared a big animal standing in the middle of the road.

A deer! I started putting on the brakes

to stop the truck. I got almost to the deer when it looked toward the woods where two more deer were coming out of the woods and ran in front of the truck. All three deer ran into the woods on the other side of the road and disappeared.

"The deer looked spooked," I said to the children, but mostly talking to myself. That's when Cody threw his hand up to his nose and started making a shewing noise.

"That smells bad, mommy," Cody said as he turned and looked at me with his hand covering his nose and mouth.

My heart started pounding when the smell met my nose and I knew that scent. It was the same smell that we all have smelled before. The same smell that was around our property so many times in the past. The smell that I will never forget!

I reached over to lock the passenger side door before I stomped on the pedal to get moving up the mountain to our home. It seemed that the road was getting darker and curvier and in my mind, was taking a very long time before we reached our driveway. But as we turned into the driveway, I felt safer than I did out on that dark mountain road.

I pulled up to the house and turned the key to stop the engine in the truck. Jake came out of the front door and down the steps to meet us and help carry groceries in. The children jumped out of the truck and ran up the steps to go watch their nightly shows on television. I came around to the side of the truck where Jake was gathering the grocery bags. He looked at me and stopped what he was doing.

"What's wrong, darling? He asked with a concerned look.

"It's a long story honey, but I will tell you when we are safe in the house," I said as I moved as fast as I could, getting all the bags I could carry in my arms.

After dinner and the children's baths, Jake and I went to relax in the front living room while Cody and Emma went to their rooms to play with their toys before they had to go to bed. I told Jake about the day's activities and how much fun we had in the city. Jake sat there patiently listening to me tell him the stories without saying a word, and I knew he was hearing me but was thinking of other things in the process. But when I told him about the drive up in the mountain, he started hanging on to every word that was leaving my mouth, and after making the story as dramatic as I could, I sat there waiting for Jake's reply.

"Please be careful when driving up the mountain at night, if you hit a deer, you could be severely injured, and that truck is the only transportation we have," Jake said as he sat back into his rocker and ran his fingers through his thick curly hair, and sighed.

I could tell that what I had told him did worry him though. He didn't like to show any kind of emotions around me because he knew that if he did, I would notice it and I would be worried or scared to stay at our farm by myself with the children when he had to work.

That night as everyone was in bed asleep, I was wide awake. The window in our bedroom had been left open half way to let some cool night air in. As I laid there, I could hear the strange yells coming from the woods that seemed so far away from the house. But after a while, I drifted off to sleep listening to the rhythm of the screams of the night.

I awoke early the next morning when I felt Jake moving in the bed. I remembered that he said that he was taking off work to harvest the fields and I felt so happy that he was not getting up to leave for work.

I rolled over on my side facing Jake and placed a gentle kiss on his forehead.

"I need to get up and start on the fields," Jake said as he began to get up from the bed.

"I'll go get breakfast started," I told him as I was already up and leaving the bedroom heading down the stairs to the kitchen.

As I walked into the kitchen, I turned on

the light and made my way to the kitchen window to open the curtains for the natural light to come in, I noticed the back door and I froze in my tracks!

I could not believe what I was looking at! The back door was wide open! I knew that the night before, as I did every night, I had made sure that all the doors were shut and locked. How could the back door be left open?

I turned to run back up the stairway to find Jake when I ran right into him coming into the kitchen.

"Whoa, what's the matter?" Jake said as I ran into his arms.

In a panic, I tried to tell Jake about the open door. He started walking toward the back of the kitchen, and went out on the back porch and looked at the back of the house. Then came back in, closed the door and said he couldn't find anything out of the way. But that still didn't relieve my worries about the back door being open or who opened it when we were sleeping.

After Jake and the children had been fed, I started to investigate the back of the house myself. What if Jake missed something? I wanted to know who or what was trying to break into the house while we were asleep.

After investigating and not finding anything either, I went down and sat down in the rocking chair on the back porch. I watched Cody and Emma play in the sand box in the back yard close to the porch. I would also watch Jake on his tractor harvesting the fields. As the fields were being cleared, the happier I became, and I knew we were that much closer to our future.

After watching Jake harvest the fields for a little while, I took the children to the front of the house with their pumpkins that they picked out the day before. We picked out a spot by the front steps to decorate with the fall décor. The children and I had a fun time gathering leaves to make a scarecrow with one of Jake's old overalls. We filled the overalls with all the leaves we could stuff in them, and Cody wanted to use his pumpkin as the head. Cody and Emma also wanted to draw the face on the pumpkin of the scarecrow instead of carving it, which was fine by me for I would have to do the job of gutting it and the carving. After the drawing of the face, the children were happy with the masterpiece that they had created, though it did look a little creepy to me.

When we were finished with decorating the front of the house, it was time for Emma's nap. I took the children to the house to put her down in her crib, with Cody following me, telling me that he was a big boy now and didn't need a nap.

With Emma down for her nap, Cody and I went to the kitchen to prepare lunch. Cody enjoyed helping me with the chores around the farm and preparing the kitchen table for lunch was a big deal for him, and I kept thinking about how both of my children were growing up so fast.

By the third day of Jake clearing the

crops, he was finished with gathering the wheat and corn. With the fields being cleared, I could see the tree line in the back of the property again.

"Do you want to go exploring in the woods, sweetie? Jake asked as he came from behind while I was looking out the back door to the tree line.

"We haven't explored the woods that are on this side of the house before," he said, pointing to the woods on the side of the house opposite of the barn side.

"Do you think it is safe to go out in the woods right now? I asked while looking at Jake, waiting on his reply

"Sure, why wouldn't it be? He said as he walked past me and out to the back porch.

"I'll bring the shotgun with us, so we'll be safe" Jake said as he walked to the edge of the bare corn field, looking out at the tree line in the back of the property.

I called for Cody and Emma to come put their shoes on and told them we were going on an adventure out in the woods. The children were excited to get out of the house and go walking. Secretly, I was too.

    We started walking toward the tree line on the other side of the house that we had never explored before, and I noticed how beautiful a day it was to go exploring. The wind was blowing in cooler air, and the leaves were crunching under our feet as we walked through the woods. We were talking, laughing and having a fun time while being out in the woods that we have never been before. We didn't need any paths to follow as we were making our way through the trees that were losing all their leaves. We could see for a long way into the woods and made our way through with Jake in front, Cody between Jake and me, and Emma being carried in a carrier on my back.

    We were making our way farther into the woods when Jake came to a sudden stop in front of us. I came around to Jake's side, and I stopped beside him. I looked in front of us and found that we were standing in front of a structure made of trees, brush, and limbs.

"What is that?" I asked Jake, thinking he had all the answers to the questions that I asked.

"Looks like an animal den of some sort," Jake said as he studied the structure and started to walk around it as to look for any clue to what might have made it.

The structure was about ten feet high and about fifteen to twenty feet in diameter, with small trees and limbs piled up on the sides and a bigger tree on top. I couldn't see if it was hollow inside and I didn't go around it to look to see either. Jake was the one that investigated the other side of the structure.

I started to get a little frightened of being out in the woods, and I turned to look back from where we came from and wanted to go back to the house.

As I looked back, I could see our house from where the structure was. I was surprised that we did not walk that far into the woods and this den was close to the side of the house where I could see Emma's bedroom window. That concerned me greatly and I was ready to leave the woods and go back our safety net that we call home.

As I was getting ready to tell Jake that I wanted to leave, he came from the back of the structure and told me that we needed to go now. I didn't argue with him, and we left in a hurry. All I was focused on was getting out of the woods and getting the children back to where they were safe.

As we came out of the woods, I looked toward the back porch and saw a figure walking on the other side of the house from where we were. My heart dropped into my stomach, and I shrieked, startling the children and Jake.

Jake stopped walking and aimed his shotgun at the figure, but lowered it as soon as we saw the figure waving at us. It was John!

While we were exploring the woods, Karen and John came to visit us and invited us to a fall festival that the city held each year.

"That sounds like fun," I said as I looked at the children, knowing that they would enjoy all the festivities that would be held. And I wanted to get away from the farm for a little while too.

We loaded the children into the truck and followed our neighbors down the mountain into town for a fun time out with family and friends. I was ready to be around people, and the small city had a peaceful era to it.

The festival had so many fun things to do for the children. Cody and Emma had a blast playing with all the games that were offered. From corn mazes, hay rides, to walking around to all the vendors selling all sorts of things from fall décor to candied apples, and we filled up on sugared treats to last us the entire year.

As the day turned into night, the festivities were still going strong, and I didn't want to leave the city. We all were having a fun time. So much fun that I did not think about the farm in the woods. But as they say, all good things do come to an end, and it was time to go home.

Cody and Emma were exhausted and fell asleep on the way back up the mountain. I was also exhausted, and all I could think of was getting into bed for a good night's rest.

As we followed John and Karen up the mountain, we came to our driveway first, flashed our lights as a goodbye to them and turned into our driveway, headed to our farmhouse.

As we came closer to the house, I saw something from the corner of my eye. It looked to be a big dark figure standing close to the driveway right beside a tree. When I turned to look where it was standing, there was nothing there but a huge stump. I don't remember a stump being there before, but, old trees fall all the time, and I concluded that I was exhausted, paranoid, and needed rest.

We brought the children inside the house, and I started up the stairs with Emma.

I entered her bedroom and put her in the crib. I covered her up with her favorite blanket and kissed her goodnight. I then turned toward the open window that faces the woods that we explored earlier that day, and my heart skipped a beat!

There in the woods were two red glowing eyes and they looked to be staring at me!

As I was staring back at the glowing eyes, I heard Jake coming up the stairs. I got his attention to come into the room to look to see what I was looking at, but as soon as Jake looked out the window, the glowing red eyes disappeared!

Jake looked outside from the window for a few minutes to see if he could see anything unusual. Absolutely nothing was making a sound and no glowing eyes anywhere!

"Darling, you need rest," Jake said as he put his arm around my shoulders and led me into our bedroom.

He was telling the truth. I did need the

rest, and I couldn't wait to fall into bed, snuggle up to him and fall into a deep sleep.

The next thing that I remembered was being awoken by a loud clash of thunder that rattled our windows. It was around 3:30 AM in the morning, and the fierce lightening was lighting up our bedroom from the windows. The next thing would be Cody running into our bedroom and jumping into bed with us and Emma's cries coming from her crib.

"Unbelievable," I said in a sarcastic tone, as I slowly get up out of bed to go tend to Emma as her cries were getting louder and uncontrollable.

I slowly walk into Emma's bedroom, rubbing my sleep deprived eyes and wishing that the storm could've waited for another time than at that moment. I picked her up and headed toward the rocking chair that was beside the closet doors in her room. The rain started to fall heavier and louder on top of the roof, and the lightening lit up the room, and the thunder rattled the windows of the house.

While I was rocking Emma, and praying that the storm would soon pass through the area, I had a strange feeling of being watched. I didn't have the nerve to go to the window and look out in the yard to see I could see anything strange outside. I just wanted to rock Emma back to sleep and go back to my own bed.

What seemed like hours sitting in the rocking chair, Emma had fallen back to sleep and the storm was letting up a little.

"Thank God," I said to myself as I ever so carefully put Emma back into the crib, afraid she would wake up again.

"Maybe I can get a little sleep now," I thought as I tiptoed out of her bedroom, headed toward my side of the bed and noticed that I had hardly any room to lay down. Cody was in a deep sleep and was curled up on my side of the bed, and I didn't want to wake him.

It seemed like no time had passed when I felt movement on the bed and realized that Cody was waking from his slumber. I thought that if only I could get just a little more sleep, I could face the day, and all the chores that I had to do that were waiting on me. But, of course, life is not that easy, and it was time to get up and start the day.

    The rain didn't stop the night before, and it would rain for the next few days after. The laundry was piling up because I had no place to hang them to dry and I started to think of ways to hang the clothes inside the house out of our way and for Emma not to play with them. After trying a few options, I gave up and waited until the rain had ended.

    Jake needed to go into the town to purchase feed for the animals and buy some hay for the horse to prepare for winter, and since it was raining, I didn't want to carry the children out for fear they may get sick. We stayed at the house.

    Since it had been raining for the past three days, the children and I were getting impatient for wanting to get out of the house. I went out to the covered back porch and sat down in the rocker. The children followed me with toys to play with out on the porch.

    I was watching Cody and Emma play together and thought of how nice it was to have two children that play together for a little while before they started fighting over the toys. The drenching downpour made the yard into a pond of about an inch of water, and I thought of how peaceful it was on the dry back porch.

    I started to relax a little and leaned back into the rocker and stared out into the back property by the tree line in a daydream. Suddenly, something caught my attention. Something started moving toward the open corn field. It was walking in the woods, getting closer to the harvested field!

    "What is that?" I asked myself.

    I kept watching to see if it would stop at the tree line. As I was watching the massive creature coming closer to the opening of the fields, my heart started pumping that much harder.

    Then it happened! The Bigfoot stepped

out of the tree line and started walking in the open field! I couldn't believe what I was looking at! I was frozen in place and all I could do was stare at this creature. I could not believe how huge this creature was! It had massive shoulders and a thick upper body, with very long arms, its hands were down to his knees, the whole body was covered in brown/black hair. It didn't take long to make it across the field onto the well-beaten path that goes down to the river!

    I watched the Bigfoot until it was out of my sight. I finally caught my breath, jumped up and took the children inside the house, locked the back door and sat down at the kitchen table.
My body was weak and I was uncontrollably shaken.

    "What did I Just see? Did it see us on the porch? Was that real? Are we safe in this house?" I kept asking myself, hoping and praying that Jake was on his way back from town.

    After about five minutes, I got up to

look out the kitchen windows to make sure that the creature was not coming back and getting close to the house. To my relief, I didn't see any sign of it, and I heard Jake pulling up to the house.

    I turned away from the kitchen window and sat back down at the kitchen table. I was still shaken by what I just saw. Jake came into the kitchen and saw me sitting at the table and knew something was wrong. If I wasn't busy with my chores, I would always try to meet him at the door when he came home.

    "What's wrong sweetie?" Jake asked as he opened the refrigerator door, grabbing a cold beer.

    I slowly looked up at him, with tears rolling down my cheeks, and started shaking my head, wiping the tears away with the back of my hand.

    Jake sat the drink down on the table and sat down beside me. He started rubbing my arm, with a concerned look on his face.

    "I just saw the creature that you saw

last winter," I said with shaking hands as tears flowed freely down my face.
"Where?" Jake asked.

All I could do was to point in the direction of the back fields. Jake got up from his chair and went to the kitchen window, looked out toward the tree line, turned and walked to the front room of the house and grabbed his shotgun. He then returned to the kitchen, went out the back door, and down to the empty corn field to investigate.

I watched as Jake walked down to the tree line and I prayed for his safety.

Later that evening after a dinner of homemade soup, with vegetables from our garden, and cornbread, it was time for the children's baths. After their baths, Cody and Emma would go to their bedrooms to play with their toys before bed time. Jake and I would go to the front living room to relax from the hard day's work.

Emma's bedroom was the closest room to the staircase and the sofa where I would sit to read my books were close to the stairs in the living room. I could hear the Cody and Emma playing in their bedrooms.

As I was reading a book that I had been trying to read for a while now, I heard Emma laughing and talking to someone. I thought that Cody came out of his room and into Emma's room to play with her. I smiled thinking how great it was for the children to be playing together.

When Cody came down stairs to get a drink of water, I smiled at him and thanked him for playing so nicely with Emma. The look on his face was of confusion.

"Mommy, I wasn't playing with Emma, I was in my room," Cody said, looking at me.

"Who is she talking to?" I asked.

"I don't know," Cody said as he shrugged his shoulders.

As soon as I asked Cody that question, I heard Emma laugh and said something that I couldn't understand.

I jumped up from the sofa and ran up the stairs to Emma's bedroom. As I came into the bedroom, I saw Emma standing in front of her bedroom window looking out with her hands on the glass, and laughing.

When I got closer to Emma and the window, I heard a faint growl.

I screamed for Jake, and it seemed that I couldn't move fast enough to get to Emma. I was afraid to look out the window, for knowing what I would see.

As I grabbed Emma, Jake was coming into the bedroom, with Cody following him. He headed toward the window, opened it, and looked out. He noticed that the screen of Emma's window had been pulled off and was lying on the ground.

Jake turned to go downstairs to the front door and go outside to the side of the house where the screen was laying on the ground. He picked the screen up, and the frame was bent, and the screen looked to be torn. He returned to the front room of the house with the screen while I closed and locked Emma's bedroom window.

Jake and I, along with the children, huddled in the front living room and studied the screen. I could tell that the screen had been ripped off the window and the rips were made from a sharp object.

"The big man from the woods did that mommy," Cody said as he looked at me with wide eyes.

"Cody, come here," Jake said in a very authoritative voice.

Cody obeyed his father and sat down in Jake's lap. I was anxious to hear what Cody had to say.

"What are you trying to tell us about the big man in the woods? Jake asked in a somewhat softer tone, as he looked at Cody, waiting on his reply.

"I don't know daddy. I see him sometimes walking in the yard going to the barn, sometimes," Cody said as he looked into Jakes' eyes, being as serious as a four-year-old could be.

"The next time you see him, you tell me, okay? Jake said as he put Cody down on the floor and got up to make sure that the front door was locked.

I sat on the sofa with Emma in my lap as I watched my husband, the bravest man that I know, looked defeated and frightened. What were we to do at this point?

Chapter 4: Winter 1980

Autumn had come to an end and winter weather was upon us. The leaves had fallen off the trees, and the snow would soon take the place of rain.

The last month of autumn, the weather had been very unpredictable. From severe weather with a threat of tornadoes to beautiful sunny days with crisp air to cloudy frigid days with the wind gusts up to about forty miles an hour. I didn't know from one day to the next what I should prepare for. All I was thinking about though was the holidays were coming fast, and I needed to be prepared for that.

I was in the kitchen cleaning the morning dishes from the table when the phone rang. I knew Jake was close to the phone and heard him answer it. I couldn't hear the conversation, but I knew he would tell me who it was and what they needed.

After Jake had hung up the phone, he walked into the kitchen where I was drying the morning dishes.

"My parents are coming for Christmas," Jake said as he put his arms around my waist and gently kissed my neck.

"How wonderful," I said as I stopped drying the dishes and thought I would finally have someone here with me as Jake goes into town for his job.

"They'll be here soon, will stay until the first of the year," Jake said.

Jake's parents were great people. I have always had a profound respect for them, and they showed me how much they love and appreciate the children and me. Anytime they would come to visit us was a treat for all and I could hardly wait to see them.

"They can stay in Emma's room. I will fix it up for them" I said excitedly as Jake let out a little chuckle. He could tell that I was overjoyed about his parents coming to visit.

As the days went by, it was time for Jake's parents to arrive. I had Emma's room made up for Arthur and Pearl to be as comfortable as possible. I also prayed that nothing strange and unusual would happen while they were here.

My in-laws were in a class of their own. Jake's father, Arthur, was a man a few words, a doer, and a very hard worker and Jake was just like him. Jake's mother, Pearl, was an outspoken woman with a personality that would make anyone fall in love with her. I have always admired Jake's parents and was thrilled to have them spend the holidays with my family.

As the days went on, it was getting closer to the big Christmas day. The children were getting excited, and it was time to decorate the house inside and out. This was my favorite thing to do, and now I had help. Pearl also loved the holidays and was willing to help with the décor and the children.

"Let's go cut a tree in the woods to put in the house to for our Christmas tree," Pearl said excitedly to the children.

"What a great idea!" I chimed in to help

get the children excited about going to find a tree to cut.

After volunteering the men to help us find a tree to cut and haul it home for us, Pearl, Cody, Emma, and I all jumped into her car while the men followed us in our truck and drove down the driveway, headed farther up the mountain in search of the perfect Christmas tree.

It didn't take long to find the perfect tree. As a matter of fact, we didn't have to get off the main country road that we would travel to go down the mountain into town. It was right there beside the road, and I was very happy that we didn't have to go into the woods.

We never told Jake's parents about the creature that was lurking around in the woods, especially around our farm. We didn't want them to be afraid to stay with us and hoped that nothing would happen when they would visit. But when Pearl kept saying that we need to go into the woods to find the perfect Christmas tree, I think my expressions on my face told her something different than what I was hoping.

"The trees that grow deeper in the woods are much prettier than the ones on the road" Pearl kept telling us as we prepared to cut the tree that we had picked out.

"We should go walking into the woods to find a different one" she would say as the men busy themselves cutting down the tree.

"I really like this one, Pearl," I said, trying not to sound like I was scared to go for a walk into those thick woods.

We didn't have to wait long for the tree to be cut. Before I knew, Jake and Arthur had the tree cut and loaded into the truck and was ready to go back to the house. I was very satisfied with the tree and was ready to get it home so we could decorate it.

Jake and Arthur got the tree home, squeezed it into the front door and stood it up in the front living room in front of the bay window. The tree was bigger than I thought and it would take some time to decorate it.

But we had the time, and we enjoyed every minute of it.

After we had the tree and the house on the inside as well as the outside decorated, I couldn't believe how beautiful our farmhouse was. I fell in love with it once again, and for a moment, I felt a peace fall over me and was happy that we had bought this property.

When we were finished with all the décor, it was time for bed, and I was exhausted. I knew that the next day would be full of activities. I needed to go shopping for the children's Christmas presents.

I woke early in the morning to get breakfast started for the whole family. Jake was still working in town and had to wake early to be on time to his job. Arthur was helping Jake with his chores and Pearl was helping me with the children. I felt safe with my in-laws being here while Jake went to work.

I had breakfast ready and on the table before everyone came down to join me in the kitchen. Jake ate his breakfast and had to leave for work. I waved to him as he drove down the driveway toward town.

After breakfast, Pearl helped me to clean the dishes off the table, and we settled down in the front living room to drink our morning coffee and watch the children play with their toys. I was helping Emma with her ride on toy when I heard Pearl clear her throat. I looked at her, and the look on her face concerned me.

"Is anything wrong Pearl?" I asked

"I heard knocking on the window last night," Pearl said as she gave me a puzzled look.

My heart skipped and beat, and a chill went up my spine. The look on my face must have surprised her because she paused and asked me if I was okay.

"What? I asked.

"I heard knocking on the upstairs bedroom window last night while I was trying to sleep. I know it sounds crazy because we were on the second floor of the house, but I knew I heard it a few times but was a little scared to get out of bed and Arthur was snoring beside me. I didn't want to wake him to see what the noise was" she said with a somewhat nervous chuckle.

I didn't know what to say to her. Should I tell her about the Bigfoot that was coming around our property, or just make up something? I just stared at her with my mind going crazy.

"You know, it was probably birds," she said as she leaned over and patted my knee.

"Thank you, Jesus," I thought to myself, relieved to not wanting to tell her the long story about the creature and scaring them, making them want to leave the children and me alone in these woods.

"Yes, you are probably right about that, it could have been birds," I said, as I felt terrible for not telling the truth.

But now I am in fear again. Why would it be knocking Emma's bedroom window? That scared me more than anything.

"Are we ready to go shopping? Pearl asked, looking at her grandchildren and bringing me out of my deep thoughts.

We got the children ready and put on their coats when Arthur comes in the front door after feeding the animals. He goes upstairs to change into different clothes and comes back down to drive us into town for fun filled day of shopping.

We had the best time shopping in town with Pearl and Arthur. I showed them around the small city, and we shopped in every little store that the town offered. We also stopped for lunch at the local diner where the special was turkey and dressing with mashed potatoes, green beans, and a dessert. We also took food home for Jake so I wouldn't have to cook that night. I was stuffed and happy, but it was getting late, and the children were exhausted. It was time to go back home.

After recuperating for a couple of days after the shopping spree, it was the weekend, and I was happy that Jake was off from work for a couple of days.

We invited our neighbors, John and Karen over to meet Jake's parents. Jake wanted to take his father out horseback riding with John. John had two horses, and he brought them over so that all three men would have a horse to ride.

I packed a lunch for the men to have when out riding. I could tell that Jake was excited about their day trip and I was happy to see him smile again. My heart was filling with joy as I looked around and saw our farmhouse decorated for Christmas and full of happy and loving people. I thought nothing could go wrong on this day.

After waving the men off into the woods on the back porch, I turned my attention to the women in the front room of the house where we would have a fun filled day of socializing. To my surprise, Karen never mentioned our visitors from the woods, and I was relieved not to have to tell Pearl the story on that day. But I knew that one day I would have to tell Jake's parents about it.

Later that evening the men came home from their adventure. Karen and Pearl had helped me with dinner, and we could tell that they were famished when they came into the door. In a very brief time, the food was eaten, and John was ready to leave to go back to their home. The men were exhausted, and I could tell they were ready to relax.

After the children had been in bed and Arthur and Pearl headed to their bedroom, Jake and I were getting ready for bed also. As we were making the bed to lie down, Jake started to tell me about their day trip.

To my surprise, Jake took the men to the cave that he found last summer, where he found the remains of our dog Atlas and other animal bones that were strewn around the cave.

"Why did you take them there? I asked, getting a little nervous.

"Why not? They wanted to explore the cave. I didn't think anything about it. We had an enjoyable time out there in the woods" Jake said as he laid down and pulled the covers over his body, ready for a good night's rest.

"What did Arthur think about it? Was there anything new in the cave? Did you see anything? I asked, looking at Jake and waiting on his reply.

"The cave looked just like it did back in the summer. Whatever lived there before is long gone now" Jake said as he rolled over on his left side, facing the wall and snuggled his head down into the pillow.

After I had thought about it, I felt relieved that Arthur knew about our visitors and I knew he would tell his wife. I didn't want to be the one to reveal to her about what was going on around our house and now that she knew, I could talk to someone other than Jake about my feelings about it.

The next day while everyone was downstairs, I got out of the shower and felt wonderful. I felt that a weight had been lifted off my shoulders because I knew that Pearl would be a shoulder that I could lean on and I could tell her everything. She was a wise woman, and I would listen to her advice.

I made my way down the staircase, and the first person I saw was Pearl. She was playing with Emma and her toys. As soon as she saw me coming into the front living room, she gave me a knowing smile, and the warm feeling that came over me was so overwhelming that I ran to her arms and started to cry.

Jake and Arthur took the children into town for the day while Pearl and I sat there on the sofa for a very long time as I poured my heart out with the feelings that had been bundled up inside for so long. After I had told Pearl everything that I could remember, I felt like a new woman, and my stress level had been drastically reduced.

Later that evening when the men came home with the children, Pearl and I had dinner waiting for them which consisted of fried chicken, mashed potatoes, green beans, cornbread, and a homemade dessert that was Pearl's secret recipe. It was a wonderful meal to end a wonderful day.

Christmas day had arrived and what an

exciting day it was. We invited John and Karen to come over to spend the day with us and to watch the children open their presents. The children got up early in the morning to see what Santa had brought them this year and could hardly wait to tear open all the present that sat under the big beautiful tree. Jake, Arthur, John, Karen, and I watched the children rip off the wrapping paper to reveal the new toy inside. We all were having a blast, but soon it came to an end as the last present was opened.

When all the presents were opened, the children sat and played with all their new toys allowing the adults to go on with the daily chores.

While the women headed to the kitchen to prepare for the Christmas dinner, the men went outside to feed the animals and to socialize in the barn.

I kept looking out of the kitchen

windows at the sky. It was a beautiful chilly day, but the clouds were getting thicker and darker, looking like snow clouds.

"Does anyone know the weather forecast?" I asked as I washed the dishes that I would use for mixing the homemade bread for dinner.

"No, I don't know but it is about noon, and the local news will show the weather will be coming on the television soon" Karen chimed in and started walking to turn the television on the local channel.

It wasn't long before we knew that a huge snow storm was headed our way. I walked to the barn where the men were visiting and told Jake about the storm. He started preparing the animals and making sure that they would fare well during the storm.

During our Christmas dinner, the snow started falling. It was a beautiful sight. We were gathered around the kitchen table, and after dinner, we all went to the front room of the house where Jake had prepared a fire in the fireplace. The Christmas tree was lit, and the soft glow of the lights and the fire made the room so comfortable and welcomed.

We socialized until about 9:00 PM that night when John and Karen realized that the snow was getting deeper, they decided that it was time for them to go home for fear they would get snowed in and may have to camp at our house.

We all said our goodbye's and watched John and Karen drive out of sight down our driveway. I stayed out on our front porch for a little while longer than Jake, and his parents did. I stood there watching the snow fall and thought of how beautiful the property was, and the snow was falling just perfectly.

My heart was full of peace, and I

thanked God for making a beautiful paradise that we could enjoy like this.

When I thought that nothing could ruin this perfect day, I turned to go back into the house, and as soon as I grabbed the doorknob, I heard something echo through the woods.

"WHOOP!!"

Conclusion

Anyone that has lived in the countryside knows that there are many positive perks of having a house perched in the woods. There are drawbacks too. There are wild animals that can wander into proximity of the home but usually will run away when they see humans. But when one of the drawbacks is that an unknown creature is lurking around the countryside, it becomes unbearable to live comfortably at home and very fearful to stay in the woods.

Be sure to read "Sharing the Mountain with Bigfoot, the third year." The third book will have pictures at the end of the book.

Printed in Great Britain
by Amazon